Rabén & Sjögren Bokförlag, Stockholm
http://www.raben.se

Rabén & Sjögren Bokförlag is a part of
P. A. Norstedt & Söner Publishing Group, established in 1823

Lena Arro • Catarina Kruusval

Good Night, Animals

Translated by Joan Sandin

R&S
BOOKS

Stockholm   New York   London   Adelaide   Toronto

Here come Bubble and Pearl.
They've each got a sleeping bag and a pillow.

Tonight they're going to sleep out in a tent.

It's exciting in the tent—almost like being inside a green cave.

Good thing Bubble brought his flashlight, because it's starting
to get dark outside . . . and what's making such an awful noise?
"It's only the wind in the trees," says Bubble.

Now there's another sound.
A rustling and scratching noise right by the entrance.
"It's only some mice," says Bubble.

Maybe the mice are afraid of the dark.
Better let them come in.
But now there's another sound outside the tent . . .

. . . something tiptoeing through the grass . . .

"It's only the cat who wants to come in," says Bubble.
His paws are probably cold. Better let him sleep inside
the tent, too, as long as he doesn't bother the mice.

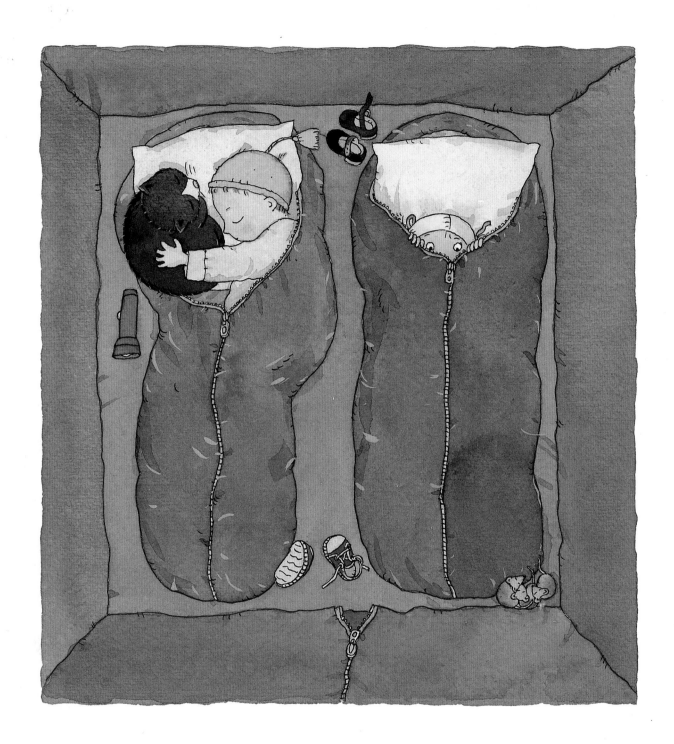

But now what's that strange noise they hear?
Something's nibbling and rustling outside.

"It's only some rabbits who want to come in,"
says Bubble.

Tonight the rabbits are a little afraid—of foxes,
and the wind that blows through the trees.
Better tuck all of them in.

What's that sound now?
Something whining and barking
and tramping around on four paws.

"It's only the dog who wants to come in," says Bubble.
He probably felt lonely out there by himself.

There must be room for a little dog in the tent.
But now what is making all that noise?

"It's only the sheep who wants to come in," says Bubble.
Probably the sheep would just like some company—
nothing odd about that.

Of course, you can always squeeze in a sheep.
Pearl hears another noise . . .

. . . a scratching and pecking from something outside.
"It's only the hen who wants to come in," says Bubble.

The hen doesn't want to sleep alone on her roost.
She likes it much better inside.

It's starting to get crowded inside the tent now.
And outside they hear a stomping and clomping.

"It's only the horse who wants to come in," says Bubble.
The horse has been grazing out under the stars,
all by himself.

Now he wants to come in with the others.
If everybody just scoots over, there will surely be enough
room for a horse.

Now it's crowded and cozy and warm in the tent.
The mice are asleep, and so is the cat.
The hen has her head tucked under her wing.
The dog is snoring in time with the horse.

The sheep is dreaming of grass.
The rabbits are dreaming of
carrots and green dandelion
leaves.
"Good night," says Pearl.
But Bubble doesn't say a thing
because he's already fallen
asleep.